MYSTERY AT POINT BEACH

~ Book 3 ~

Alien Invasion

Kate Jungwirth

Deborah Erdmann

This book is dedicated to:

The Maker of the universe

~ DE

Liam,

my youngest space explorer

~ KJ

PROLOGUE

Manitowoc County, Wisconsin, 1962

The moon was full; a beam of light streamed over the pond across the field. The elderly, small-town farmer had just finished his work for the day. Earl paused, rubbing his chin with his calloused hand. The light shone particularly bright, it seemed to him. In fact, now that he gave it careful consideration, the light wasn't actually coming from the moon. He looked up then, nearly startled out of his suspenders.

Hovering overhead was a luminous, silver cloud. A soft halo glowed around it, emitting a faint, buzzing sound. Suddenly, the cloud shot up into space, leaving a hole in the sky where a smattering of stars had been. Earl froze in his work boots. Martha would never believe it. Not in a million years.

CHAPTER 1

"Earth to Dominic. Hello?" Grandpa Bob swatted me with his Green Bay Packer cap before turning his attention back to the road.

"Sorry, GB. It's just that I'm trying to get through as many of these *Star Trek* comic books as I can. Maybe it will help solve the mystery of the strange lights and UFOs in the sky at Point Beach."

The whole spaceship thing seemed to go right over GB's head. He continued down the road at a snail's pace with his relic camper, "Nimrod," following faithfully behind.

"If you ask me, it's kooky that Mrs. Buckley thinks you're going to solve some big sci-fi scare. What does a twelve-year-old boy even know about aliens and what-not?"

I waved my comic book in his face. "Why do you think I'm studying these outer space books?" *Ughhh ...*

Sadie Buckley and her husband, Bert, are the camp hosts at Point Beach State Forest in Two Rivers, Wisconsin, where we vacation every summer. She called me last week to ask if my friends, Forest, Sailor, and I could investigate some mysterious phenomena over Lake Michigan. We consider ourselves a team of teenage detectives, having previously solved two mysteries at Point Beach, but I like to think of myself as the head of the operation.

"So, tell me again, what exactly is going on at the campground?" GB asked.

"Apparently, a meteorite crashed into the lake last week. Since then, green glowing lights keep showing up at the park, scaring away most of the campers."

"I still can't believe your mother is allowing you to miss school over this. And what about Forest and Sailor?" he said, stroking the stubble on his chin.

I suspected he was growing a beard to impress their grandma, Windsong.

"They're homeschooled, so it doesn't really matter for them, and I can make up the work when I get back." Besides, spending time with Windsong was like having a lesson on the hippie movement and nature all rolled into one.

"Can't Ranger Rick handle the UFO crisis?" GB made a slow left into the park entrance.

I laughed. "He *is* out of this world, but the campground will become a ghost town before he figures anything out." So far, Ranger Rick did not have a good track record of being helpful—if anything, he'd slow down our progress.

Even though we only had three days to solve the mystery, I was confident it would be a snap. Granted, it was now autumn, creating a little different atmosphere from our usual summer trips, but I still felt I knew the park like the back of my hand. If anything seemed out of the ordinary, I would know.

After checking in at the park office, we started to drive off, when GB made an unexpected turn.

"Stop, Grandpa Bob. You're going the wrong way. Site #127 is straight ahead."

"Sorry, Dominic. I know nothing compares to

our preferred site, but it's already taken. When you show up last-minute like this, it's first come, first serve."

I slouched in my seat. Without being positioned close to all the action on the beach, it would be a little less than ideal, but I would have to put up with it.

We meandered down the road, making our way to our site. Upon approach, it didn't look too shabby. Site #101 was secluded, surrounded by towering evergreens.

I jumped out of the truck before it came to a stop, excited to see the huge yard. "Look, GB. The fire pit is way back in the woods!"

GB shifted into park and joined me. "See, Dominic? When life throws you a lemon ..."

"I know. You make lemonade. You need to come up with some new material."

"Will do. Now help me get things situated before you go running off."

"I'll be right there." I walked into the woods to survey the fire pit situation. It was really private ...

and dark. The trees were so dense, sunlight couldn't even filter through. Out of the corner of my eye I thought I saw a bush moving from one tree to another. When I turned to get a better look, it stopped. The hairs on the back of my neck stood up.

"GB!"

"What's wrong?" He came running into the woods.

"I … I thought I saw something."

"Well? What was it?" GB wheezed, pulling out his handkerchief to mop his forehead.

"It was … it was … a spider." I decided to keep quiet about the traveling bush. Knowing GB, he'd call Mom and worry her. Maybe insist she take me to a psychiatrist.

"Land sakes, Dominic! You gave me a near-heart attack over a spider?" GB shook his head as he walked back to the truck.

Whew, that was a close one. Good thing I know when to shut my mouth.

We went about setting up Nimrod, which in-

cluded unloading Tupperware containers full of
Mom's chocolate chip cookies, fresh fruit, marshmallows, and cheese curds, along with our pillows. For
being in a big hurry to leave, I was glad GB packed all
the essentials.

"Here, let me help you with that." I reached for
the cooler he was lifting from the cab and opened the
lid, taking out an Orange Crush.

"You call that helping?" GB frowned.

"Well, yeah. I got this one for you. Plus, I'm making it lighter, see?" I opened the lid again, grabbing
another Crush for myself.

"How would I ever manage without you?" GB
asked, placing the cooler by the picnic table.

I was beginning to wonder that myself.

"I really need to look for the rest of the gang. Can
you catch up with me later?" When GB nodded his approval, I took off on my lime-green Trek.

Turns out we were just around the corner from
the camp hosts. I used my hand brakes, swerving into
the Buckley's site, gravel flying beneath my wheels. I

noticed they had added a few more plastic flamingos to their over-the-top yard décor.

Sadie Buckley had just walked out of her camper, clad in a gaudy jungle dress of brown and emerald green; her blue hair stacked in rollers. Bert followed, wearing a faded, red-checked flannel shirt, nearly getting his nose smacked by the swinging screen door behind her. Their white miniature poodle, Sprinkles, dashed toward me, barking her head off.

"Hello, Martin." Sadie steadied her eyes on me from behind thick glasses. "Albert and I were just talking, wondering what was taking you so long."

I came to the conclusion a long time ago that she would never remember my name.

"Hi, Mrs. Buckley. Hi, Mr. Buckley." I got off my bike, putting down the kickstand. "Thanks for calling us, and sorry about the delay—GB had to get Nimrod out of storage. I'm ready to take the case now."

"Good!" Sadie clapped her hands. "I knew you'd help."

"Okay, now start from the beginning." I prepared to take some mental notes. "Tell me everything that happened. Don't leave anything out."

Sadie's tone was troubled. "Well, as I was telling you over the phone, a few days ago Bert and I noticed that Sprinkles was not her usual self. She was very agitated; howling and waking us up."

"She wouldn't let us sleep," Bert reiterated.

"Suddenly, a loud 'boom' crashed through the woods, shaking the walls of our camper." Sadie's hands darted about like small birds. "Everyone at the park heard it."

"I heard it, too!" Bert's eyes grew big as saucers.

Even with his hearing aids he can't hear anything, so this was monumental.

"We were told that a meteorite landed right in Lake Michigan from outer space, but that's not all." She pointed toward the beach. "We saw a spooky, green glowing light over by the lake the last few days."

"Did you tell Ranger Rick?"

"The ranger won't listen. He said it's probably just swamp gas." Bert removed his hat from his bald head, swatting a fly with it.

I crinkled my nose. "What's swamp gas?"

"It's common at Point Beach because we're surrounded by swamp. Sometimes the vapor catches fire and glows."

"So, there could be a logical explanation, then?" I was afraid of even the slightest possibility that this whole mystery was a false alarm. Especially considering the Buckleys were not always the most reliable witnesses.

"If you ask me, this is something supernatural—extraterrestrials, no doubt." Bert folded his arms. "They've been here before, you know. Some people just want to keep it top secret."

"Maybe they're attracted to your campsite decorations." I nodded in the direction of the flamingos. "What's with the blue ones? I thought flamingos were supposed to be pink."

Sadie smiled, smoothing her dress over her hips. "Actually, their feathers can be various colors, depending on their diets. Don't you just love them? I sent Bert to the store to pick up some more. You can never have enough flamingos."

"Very cool. I bet they're just flying off the shelves, heh heh." I climbed back on my bike, ready for more investigating. "See you later. I need to go find Forest and Sailor now."

I tried to imagine what it would look like if they filled their entire site with colored, stick-legged plastic birds—Jurassic Park frozen in time. I wondered if Sadie's hair rollers were wound too tight.

I had just turned the corner, when I spied the strangest spacecraft on wheels that I had ever seen. It was a silver van with antennas sticking out every-where; revolving scanners mounted to the roof. Images of aliens with gray bodies and big, black eyes were cus-tom-painted on each side.

I hid behind a bush while it passed by. *Weird.*

CHAPTER 2

"What are you doing in that bush?" GB stopped his bike alongside me, cocking an eyebrow. "More spiders?"

My heart skipped a beat. "Grandpa Bob ... it's only you." A few minutes sooner and he would've blown my cover.

Speechless, I brushed the leaves off my jeans, hauled my bike back out to the edge of the road, and started pedaling behind him. At a distance, I spotted what had to be Windsong's kiwi-green RV on site #125.

"Hey, boys!" Windsong stepped out of her camper looking colorful in a tie-dyed sundress; an orange and yellow-flowered hair band held back the waves of her long, silver-streaked hair.

"Greetings, meh lady." GB bowed.

Windsong curtsied. "Greetings to you, meh lord.

To what do I owe the pleasure?"

Was it time for the nursing home, already?

"My goodness, Bobby, are you growing a goatee? I really dig it."

GB blushed, a goofy smile plastered on his face.

I cut to the chase. "The two of you do realize we have a mystery on our hands? We need to get to work."

"No problem, Dominic. But wait, I brought you a present—maple-flavored marshmallows! I knew you'd get a kick out of them." Windsong plucked the bag from her picnic basket.

"What do you say?" GB gave me the stink eye.

"Thank you, Windsong." My cheeks flushed.

"You're welcome. If you're looking for Forest and Sailor, they're waiting for you out back."

That could only mean they were in our secret fort.

My Nike's filled with sand as I climbed the hill behind the campsite. The golden sun warmed my skin as I neared the crest, reminding me how glad I was for the Indian summer. Mom had packed my long underwear and wool socks, but I had a feeling I wouldn't need to unpack them.

Someone tore down most of our fort the last time we were here. Only a few sticks were left behind to hold our meeting place together, making it easy to spot Forest and Sailor through the gaps.

"Hi, guys!" I ran to the fort, peering inside. Forest was dressed in his usual high-end attire—a tight T-shirt and khaki cargo shorts. I was surprised to see his sun-bleached hair was much shorter now, but he still wore his bangs long, which swept across his forehead, partially covering his eyes.

Sailor hadn't changed a bit. Her fluorescent pink and green blouse gave off the desired effect, nearly blinding me. She was still skinny as a toothpick, her straw-colored hair down to her waist.

"Dominic!" She waved both hands at me. "Can you believe we got called on assignment?"

Forest leaned back on his elbows and crossed his legs. "I feel like we should be getting paid for this, especially since we came all the way from Chicago."

"I'm getting out of school. That's payment enough," I said. "My mom wasn't thrilled, though. Did Grandma Windsong freak out when you told her you were needed at Point Beach to help solve a mystery?"

"Nah, she was cool." He dangled his right flip-flop off his toes.

"And besides," Sailor chimed in, "our mom is dating some tourist agent guy now, so with us gone, they can see the highlights of the Windy City on some architectural river boat cruise. Even though we lived there our whole lives, he claims there's more to see than meets the eye." She blew a big bubble from the wad of grape gum she was chewing.

"I've always dreamed of Chicago," I said.

"Really?" Sailor jumped up, hitting her head on the roof. "You should come and visit us sometime — you and Grandpa Bob!"

"No. I don't want to go there. I just want to dream about it." *GB in Chicago? The city would eat him alive.* "So, have you guys noticed anything out of the ordinary at the campground?"

"Yeah. We're the only ones here." Forest snapped a twig in half.

"It's like a ghost town," Sailor's blue eyes darkened, her voice dropping to a whisper, "except for site #127. We went looking for you at your usual site but found someone else there. They have a van with aliens on it, and a red VW Beetle."

"Their car isn't red, it's green. And it's definitely not a VW, it's a BMW—big difference," Forest argued.

"It's red, Forest. You're color blind, remember? And so what if I don't know the kinds of cars. At least I know my colors," she crowed.

"If someone's vehicle ever gets stolen, you two better hope you're together to give the police report." I laughed. "Anyway, I'm sure I saw the van you're talking about. Do you have any idea what they're up to?"

"No, but we can find out." Sailor dashed out of the fort, leading the way to the top of the dune behind site #127. The same alien van I saw earlier was parked next to a sporty car. It was most definitely a red BMW.

One mystery solved—one to go.

We crouched low behind a patch of junipers. A petite woman with crimson hair and smart-looking, black-framed glasses was sitting at the picnic table, studying a large map of the campground. Behind her stood a young man dressed in a camouflage, sleeveless T-shirt with a buzz-cut hairstyle and black combat boots. He was tinkering with a camera on a tripod; a stick of beef jerky lodged in his cheek.

"Quinn, look at this! I found the perfect place to shoot your YouTube video." She pointed to a location on the map.

The guy named Quinn washed down his last bite with a Monster Energy drink as he headed toward the picnic table. He leaned in closer, nodding his head.

"Oh yeah, Wanda, good work. Just wait 'til this video goes viral. When I prove the existence of aliens, people won't be calling me a nut case anymore."

"It's unbelievable how the list of eyewitnesses keeps piling up. Listen to this Trip Advisor review that came in today." Wanda began to read out loud from her phone:

She looked up, her eyes squinting in the bright sun. "Like I told you before, you're definitely in the right place. I'll see if I can contact the reviewer and set up a live interview for the documentary."

"Excellent! See, Wanda? People are finally realizing that aliens are legit."

"How many followers do you have, anyway?"

"Last time I checked it was over 2000, but I expect they will outnumber the stars in the sky by the time my work here is finished." Quinn crushed the Monster can under his boot and began loading his camera equipment.

I motioned Forest and Sailor to follow me back to the fort, where I took a seat under the roof of driftwood twigs that crisscrossed overhead. "Looks like this guy is some kind of alien hunter. That means the news about the meteorite and the mysterious lights must've spread. It's possible they even made headlines by now."

"Yeah, this is bigger than we imagined ..." Sailor stared out at the lake, deep in thought.

Forest pulled a bag of M&M's out of his pocket, toying with the colored candies. "You know something? That Quinn guy looks familiar. I've seen him before."

I glanced at Forest and Sailor. "We need to keep an eye on those two. Pass the M&M's."

CHAPTER 3

Back at site #125, an oldies tune was playing on the radio. GB sat on a lawn chair, relaxing under a bright string of lanterns, while Windsong worked on a crossword puzzle at the picnic table.

"Looks like there's going to be a mushroom walk tomorrow." GB held open the article in the *Friends of Point Beach* newsletter.

"Sounds groovy. Count me in!" Windsong gave a thumbs up as he continued to look over the columns.

"And I see they're even setting up a high-powered telescope to view the stars and planets tonight. I think we all should go."

"I sure hope there's not another meteor coming our way. Nimrod's old canvas walls wouldn't stand a chance," Forest teased.

"Or maybe we'll catch a glimpse of those eerie lights!" My heart raced. "I'm starting to believe in the alien theory — the Buckleys have me convinced."

"Groovy, I've always had an interest in the cosmos." Windsong grabbed a pencil that was tucked behind her hair band and opened her puzzle book.

I believe it — she's spaced out already.

Grandpa Bob, on the other hand, wouldn't be so easily persuaded. Science fiction wasn't up his alley, especially when I tried to get him to watch old *Star Trek* episodes.

"Um … Dominic, I hate to break it to you, but the camp hosts aren't playing with a full deck, in case you haven't noticed." Forest reached into a cooler by the picnic table for a bottle of water.

"Forest Everly! I will not have you being disrespectful of your elders." Windsong lightly tapped his backside with her puzzle book. "Sadie and Bert Buckley are the sweetest couple you'll ever meet."

Poor Forest. His face turned red as a beet.

"Why don't you kids find something to eat before we leave," Windsong suggested. "The sky's getting dark already."

"Don't mind if I do," I said, walking into their RV. Colorful, beaded-curtains were strung as a partition in front of the master bedroom, and a row of neon-colored peace signs and floral banners were arranged over the kitchen cabinets.

"Wow, this place looks even more psychedelic than it did last year!" It was so kaleidoscopic, I wondered how they even slept at night.

"Since Windsong camps so much now, she wanted to make it homier." Sailor reached for a banana from a hanging basket.

"Uh, yeah. I think she pulled it off," I mumbled.

Forest stuck his nose into the small, dorm-sized refrigerator. "Do you want spinach and goat cheese wraps, or avocado and hummus quesadillas?"

I resisted the urge to pinch my nose shut. "Let's just head out." I grabbed a banana.

Billions of stars shone brightly overhead. Point Beach was a great place to view the night sky—out in the middle of nowhere, far away from the city lights.

A man in a black watch cap with a crooked nose was operating the refractor telescope. He excitedly picked out clusters of constellations as we gathered by the nature center with a few other spectators.

Finally, it was my turn to use the telescope. I carefully looked into the eyepiece that was attached to the optical tube. It was easy to focus in on the craters of the full moon, but trying to spot signs of life beyond earth was not so simple. This is where having an expert around could turn out to be a huge advantage.

"Did you happen to come across any sightings of green lights flashing over Point Beach lately?" I asked the astronomer.

"As a matter of fact, I did. About a week ago, there was a meteorite—it burned like a bright green shooting star before landing in Lake Michigan."

"See, Dominic, there's always a logical explanation for everything," GB concluded.

"But Sadie claimed the green lights keep reappearing," I argued. "How often do shooting stars land in the same place *and* scare off all the campers?"

"Now, that's a stellar question," the man said, rubbing his chin. "Meteor showers are common, but they usually don't draw that kind of attention. To create a flash of light as you described, it would take a huge piece of space rock consisting mostly of metal that burns green, such as copper, for instance."

"Could a spaceship do this?" Sailor asked him.

"The probability seems unlikely, but not to the mind of flexible thinkers," he conceded. "Perhaps, you'll be one of the first to find out."

"If we're looking for them, they're looking for us," Windsong said, taking a second peek through the telescope lens.

I tried to envision an alien spaceship using the top of the lighthouse as a landing port. *Now, that would take some talent.* When we were through, the astronomer packed up his gear and headed inside.

"Well, guys, I guess we can scratch off any natural reasons for the disturbances at Point Beach." Forest kicked a stick to the curb.

"That leaves either a man-made or supernatural explanation." I no sooner spoke, when the alien van pulled into the parking lot; green underglow lights illuminating the pavement beneath its metal frame.

"Calling all UFO fanatics ..." A man's squeaky voice broadcast over a megaphone that spun in circles on top of the roof; creepy synthesizer music played in the background.

"This is Captain Quinn from Sci-Fi-Wisconsin. Unusual lights have been reported over Lake Michigan. An investigation is underway to determine whether another life form is targeting Point Beach. If you have any information or if you encounter aliens—notify me immediately at campsite #127. Over and out."

The alien van stopped, and the side door flipped up. Wanda stepped out wearing cheetah-print leggings, a sleek vest and knee-high boots. She was shooting a video of Quinn as he marched through the parking lot in a full length, black trench coat. Why he wore sunglasses at night was beyond me.

"These people seem to be one coil short of a slinky. Don't they know that Halloween is next month?" GB shook his head in disbelief.

"Hey, wait a minute … now I remember this guy!" Forest made a mad dash for the van.

"You know, that's not an ice cream truck," Windsong called after him.

The rest of us walked over to see what the fuss was about.

"Guys, I can't believe I didn't recognize him right away. It's Captain Quinn. I saw him on YouTube a while back. When it comes to aliens, he's the expert!" Forest gushed.

"Is that right?" GB walked up to the van, peeking inside. "This is some getup. What are all these antennas and doohickeys for?" he asked, pointing to the roof.

Quinn removed his sunglasses. "These 'doohickeys,' my good fellow, are various decoders and radar for detecting extraterrestrial disturbances, as well as a camera to record sky lights and atmospheric changes."

"Cool." I peeked in alongside GB.

"Perhaps you've seen episodes of my popular science fiction YouTube station?" Quinn asked.

"Never heard of it," GB admitted.

"You should tune in. My specialty is to further the awareness of aliens. You can even track UFO sightings in Wisconsin on my website: SCI-FI-WI.com."

"Our grandchildren are also investigating aliens at Point Beach," Windsong said.

"Well, Ma'am, this job isn't for amateurs." He looked us over. "Only a small percentage of the reports that come in are actual alien encounters. It takes a trained eye to know the difference."

Quinn turned his attention to the small crowd that had gathered while Wanda trailed him with the video camera.

"This is an exciting time to be on the planet, people. The signs of extraterrestrial life forms are all around us. I'll be at Sputnikfest for the next two days,

so head over to Manitowoc. You don't want to miss it."
Sliding his sunglasses back on, he began handing out business cards.

Right on cue, Ranger Rick pulled into the lot.

CHAPTER 4

The DNR truck came to a screeching halt. Out came Ranger Rick, slamming the door behind him. We stepped back, leaving Wanda and Quinn to contend with the ranger, who wasn't too happy, judging by the scowl on his face.

Wanda focused the camera on Quinn as he walked into the limelight. "Greetings, Ranger. Glad you could join us."

"Listen, bub, this is a civilized campground. We don't tolerate your kind around here." Ranger Rick eyed the alien images on the van. "You and your sideshow best be moving along."

"Excuse me, sir, but I have an obligation to my SCI-FI-WI followers to investigate all reports of paranormal activity. Point Beach appears to be a hot spot, in case you haven't noticed."

"There's nothing paranormal around here except

you, loony-toon." Ranger Rick crossed his arms. "The only alien species we need to worry about are gypsy moths and silver carp."

"Tell that to the hundreds of people who reported seeing UFOs along Lake Michigan. How can that many people be wrong?" Quinn rebutted.

"Perhaps the ranger can shed some light on the conspiracy that took place at Point Beach back in 1962?" Wanda cornered him, zooming in the camera.

Ranger Rick looked stupefied. "There's no such thing, lady. I have no clue what you're talking about."

"So, you deny the UFO cover-up?" She tightly pursed her lips. "We've heard some very compelling testimony from one of your campers here …."

"Now, now, shut that thing off," Ranger Rick sputtered as he removed his hat, holding it up to block the shot.

"Have it your way," Quinn retorted, "but you'll be begging for my help if aliens come after you." With that, Quinn and Wanda got into the van and drove off.

"That was awesome!" Sailor twirled like a ballerina, stopping mid-circle as Ranger Rick approached.

"Step aside, Rainbow Brite." He rudely brushed past her. "What are you three mischief-makers doing here? Shouldn't you be in school?"

"The Buckleys asked us to investigate the strange lights that are scaring off all your campers." I blinked rapidly.

The ranger's nostrils flared. "Ah, I see what you're up to." He placed his hands on his hips. "You're trying to create a mystery to solve where there is none. Aliens don't exist—end of discussion."

"But Ranger …" I objected, "it's not us. You should be watching the Sci-Fi people on site #127. They're the ones talking about a conspiracy."

"But nothing. You have to get up pretty early in the morning to fool *this* ranger. If I hear any more talk about conspiracies or Martians, you'll be kicked out of the park right along with those SCI-FI-WI jokers."

GB clenched his fists into a ball. "For your information, these kids received a commendation from the local police department for their help in solving crimes at this park. Why, I oughta …"

"Now, Bob Dorsey, don't get your knickers in a knot. All I'm doing is trying to prevent mass hysteria, and I'd 'preciate it if you keep your grandson under wraps, is all."

With that, Ranger Rick tore out of the parking lot as quickly as he had entered it.

"Geez, I'm glad that's over," I groaned.

"Yeah, but can someone tell me what a conspiracy is?" Sailor's eyebrows scrunched together.

"You see, dear, it's a kind of plot to cover-up something you don't want people to know about," Windsong explained. "Like when you and Forest hide your lima beans in your napkins at dinner."

"Oh …" Sailor squirmed.

"Well, I've had enough excitement for one night. The only conspiracy I'm worried about is the one that's preventing me from getting some sleep," GB said.

"You mean we're awake? It feels like some weird kind of nightmare to me." Forest laughed.

"Yes, and don't forget tomorrow we're doing the

mushroom walk with the park's nature guide."

"Grandpa Bob! We don't have time for your fancy mushroom walk. We have our work cut out for us the way it is."

Windsong ruffled my hair. "Sorry, Dominic, but I promised Forest and Sailor's mom they'd learn a thing or two while we're here. Given the choice between nature or aliens, she'd probably choose nature."

"I've never gone mushroom picking before. It sounds exciting!" Sailor enthusiastically cheered.

I'd rather pop bubble wrap.

"See you in the morning, guys." I headed back to our site with GB leading the way. Once we got inside our rustic little camper, Grandpa Bob didn't waste any time climbing into bed and falling asleep. Unfortunately, I had too much going on in my squirrel cage to do the same.

I stretched the white flannel covers up to my neck, staring at the ceiling. Maybe some fresh air would help. Pulling back the zipper on the flap that covered my screened-in window, I looked up into the night sky, attempting to remember where all the con-stellations were. I had just found the Big Dipper, when a probing light materialized right before my eyes.

What was that?

I squinted, trying to make out where the light was coming from, but I couldn't see either end. Then it vanished, like the teleport beam on *Star Trek*.

My detective's intuition told me I needed to get a closer look. I tiptoed from my cot to the door. Luckily, GB's snores were loud enough to overpower a bugle, allowing me to slip out into the darkness without waking him.

Flashlight in hand, I walked the road lined with empty campsites down to the beach. Lake Michigan's foamy waves crept up to my toes as I watched the night sky, waiting for the green cosmic light to reap-pear over the foggy abyss on the shore.

Looking upward, I blinked a few times, rubbing my eyes to make sure what I saw was real.

A small whiz of light darted back and forth overhead. It hovered motionless, only to pick up speed almost instantly, shifting in another direction. I stood, mesmerized, watching the shiny, dancing light, until it disappeared.

Could it be a UFO?

All at once, the wind picked up over the lake, and the long grass began to rustle. Something told me I shouldn't be here anymore. Before I could turn around, I heard a branch snap ahead of me. Someone or *something* was coming my way.

Instinctively, I crouched down beside an uprooted tree, peering over its dead limbs. Out of nowhere, a blinding green light probed through the mist, causing me to shield my eyes. It was radiating from a dark figure holding a large, glowing lens. Beads of sweat dripped from my forehead. I stayed still until the figure passed by. *Whew, that was close.*

Taking a deep breath, I suddenly wondered how long it'd been since I changed my socks. Something literally stunk to high heaven.

Time to get out of here. I started to get up just as a large creature brushed past the back of my legs.

"SQUEEEEE … squee squee …"

Holy … pig?

I dove further under the tree roots, worried the big, fat pig would trample me. The animal snorted a few more times before ambling behind a brush pile.

Thinking it was finally safe to come out, I carefully made my way back to the campsite. All around, I noticed an eerie, green mist rising into the silent treetops. The thought of an alien invasion scared me to the core.

CHAPTER 5

"Rise and shine, sleepy head." GB gently shook me.

I threw back my warm blankets. "I gotta go meet Forest and Sailor. There's been a break in the case."

"A break in the case? Did you come up with something in your dreams?"

"This might sound like a dream to you, Grandpa, but last night I couldn't sleep, so I went outside. You would not believe what I saw!"

"Hold that thought. I need to flip the panny cakes. How many do you want?"

"I'll take ten."

"I'd like to see you try. Ten bucks says you can only eat eight," GB wagered.

I grabbed the orange juice out of the fridge and headed to the table, sliding past the familiar rip in the red vinyl seat cushion that GB was too cheap to fix.

"So, anyway, I went for a walk over by the lake,

and all of a sudden a pig shows up—a *pig*, GB!"

GB spun around so fast the pancake on his spatula flew into the wall. "That does sound like a dream. No way there's a pig at this campground, and you know better than to wander off by yourself in the first place," he sighed, reaching for the paper towels.

"I saw it, Grandpa. Believe me."

I refrained from mentioning the UFO and the green light. I might not get any pancakes at this rate.

I poured a mound of maple syrup over the stack he set before me, digging my fork and knife into it. After those were gone, I loaded three more onto my plate.

"Slow down, Dominic. You'll get a bellyache." GB poured more batter onto the griddle.

"Hey, you made these ones bigger on purpose," I groaned, swallowing pancake number eight.

"Ready to give up yet?" GB flipped a pancake with a spatula while my stomach did a few flips of its own.

"Bring it on." I took a gulp of milk, summoning up the adrenaline I had left over from last night. Even though my pajama bottoms had become painfully tight, I shoveled them in until I finished off the final two, raising my empty plate like a trophy.

"Ta-da!"

"Very impressive, kiddo." GB reached in his pocket for his wallet. "Here's your ten bucks. Now hurry up and get dressed. It's time to go meet the gang for the mushroom walk."

I slipped a grey, thermal shirt over my head, and squeezed into the most elastic pair of pants I had packed. Then I brushed the sugar off my teeth, wetting down my thick, brown hair before combing through my cowlick. It was a challenge trying to determine if I looked presentable in the warped mirror that hung on a nail over the sink. It distorted my reflection, sort of like those mirrors at a circus.

Windsong, Forest and Sailor were already inside the nature center when we got there. Windsong was talking to an elderly hippie with long, brown hair and a scruffy white beard, in knee-high boots. She was being her usual, animated self. The nature guy seemed quite taken with her.

"What's with Willie Nelson?" GB muttered as we walked over and joined them by the center table.

"Guys, over here." I pulled Forest and Sailor off to the side. "Big news! Everything's true—I saw lights flashing over the lake last night."

"Are you sure it wasn't coming from the light-house?" Forest asked. "It got pretty foggy, you know."

"It wasn't that," I insisted. "The light was green, and it beamed straight up into the sky. They were coming from a UFO, and …" I rubbed my neck. *Here goes nothing.* "I know you won't believe me, but after I saw the lights, I was chased down by a wild pig!"

"Haha! Were you walking in your sleep again?" Forest held his sides, laughing along with Sailor.

"Come on, you guys. I saw a pig. I swear."

"Hogwash. Not buying it." Forest was having a heyday until the nature guy called everyone's attention to the front of the room.

"Hello. I'm Norman Lates—naturalist extraordi-naire. Looks like only a small crowd today, but I'm glad you could join me for the mushroom walk."

Forest poked me in the ribs. "Norman seems like he's a really fun guy. Get it? Fun-gi?"

I wasn't in the mood for Forest's bad jokes. I just wanted to hunt around the campground for clues, not take up half a day listening to lectures and looking at fungus. I get enough of that looking at GB's toenails.

Norman gestured toward a few posters on the wall. "Some mushroom species you'll see today might include meadow mushrooms, chanterelles, oyster mushrooms, shaggy manes, and bear's head tooth mushrooms."

"Mushroom stew, mushroom gravy, mushroom pizza ..." Forest did his impersonation from the *Forrest Gump* movie, but the mushroom guy didn't see the humor in it.

"Why, yes—when prepared correctly, mushrooms can be used to create all kinds of rare, organic delicacies," Norman continued, captivating Windsong as she hung on every word.

"The only *delicacy* I've ever tasted is SPAM. Right

GB?" I gave him a nudge. It's his favorite.

"Humpf." GB grumbled under his breath.

"Grab a bucket if you need one and let's head out the back door here, folks. Stay on the path and be careful not to trample any mushrooms underfoot." Norman exited the building with Windsong hot on his heels.

GB shoved his hands in his pockets.

We each grabbed a bucket by the handle and followed behind the grown-ups, stopping by decomposed logs and old, moss-covered trees to look for anything that resembled a type of fungus. As we got deeper into the woods, a loud, croaking sound caught our attention.

"Now, folks, you'll notice the frogs are getting quite boisterous. When you hear them start making a racket like that, it usually means we're getting some rain." Norman pointed to a swamp on the right where the sound was coming from. "They're actually calling out to potential mates because they lay their eggs in the water. When the small ponds fill up with water, they become perfect nurseries."

"How romantic!" Windsong placed her hand on her heart. "Isn't it, Bobby?" She turned, smiling at GB. He rolled his eyes and kept walking.

"You know, if you keep rolling your eyes, GB, they're gonna stick that way." I don't think my comment helped matters. He looked even more annoyed.

Sailor stopped short, causing Forest to stumble behind her. "Hey, you guys, I found a bumper crop over here!" She stood in front of a cluster of round, white mushrooms.

"Yeah, but what if they're poisonous? I don't think we can eat this kind," I said.

"What—you mean some mushrooms can kill you?" Sailor gasped.

"More for the rest of us, then." Forest reached for the biggest one.

"Ah, ha. These fellows are called giant white puffballs." Norman picked one, slicing it down the middle with his pocketknife. The inside was solid white, like a marshmallow. "These are safe to eat, but once they go bad, they turn green inside."

"Cool!" Forest furiously yanked mushrooms out of the ground, like it was a contest.

We all picked some. They were so big that they quickly filled our buckets. There was nothing left for us to do but listen to Norman's boring lecture.

"Did you know mushrooms contain fiber, protein, vitamin D, vitamin B, and potassium? Not to mention, they're a great source of selenium which strengthens the immune system and helps reduce cancer and other illnesses. Also, the penicillin antibiotic is derived from mushrooms, and ..."

"I have a question," I said.

"About mushrooms?" He slid the knife back into his chest pocket.

"No, about swamp gas. Is it possible for the gas around here to burn and cause green lights in the sky?"

"Kid, where did you get such a crazy idea?" Norman leaned on his walking stick. "Are you confusing the alien sightings with swamp gas? I've seen those sky lights myself, and it ain't no swamp gas."

"To be honest," he lowered his voice, "you folks aren't safe at Point Beach. I'm high tailing it out of here myself after this tour. I only stayed because I signed up to be a guide for the walk a few months ago, and there was no backing out."

Norman led us deeper into the woods. The mushrooms were getting scarcer now, and it felt as though we were only going in circles. He suddenly stopped, turning toward us as we crossed to the next trail.

"Well, folks, that's it for the mushroom walk. If you follow the trail back to the road, you'll end up at the camp host site. I hope you'll take my advice and vacate the park." He nodded curtly, continuing on his way.

We all stopped behind him, looking at each other quite bewildered.

What was going on here?

"Well, that was certainly strange." Windsong watched as he disappeared around the bend. "So, the alien conspiracy continues?"

"Apparently." GB turned back, with all of us following suit.

In the distance, I heard a rumble. Gears shifted noisily as Bert and Sadie pulled up in their golf cart.

"Kids, come quick!" Mrs. Buckley called from the road. "The ranger's gone missing. We think he might have been abducted!"

CHAPTER 6

"Are you serious? Ranger Rick's been abducted?" My bucket tipped, causing a few mushrooms to tumble out.

"We can only hope," Forest jeered.

"What happened, Mrs. B?" I asked, as we dashed toward the golf cart.

"Bert and I were going for a walk this morning when we saw a big beast moving in the woods. It went after Sprinkles and attacked her." Sadie began doting on Sprinkles who had a scrape on her paw. "Mama's poor baby," she kept saying, before she finally got back to telling us about the incident.

"When I went to get a closer look, the creature was gone, but I noticed Sprinkles had dug up a walkie-talkie lying in the weeds by an uprooted tree."

"It belongs to Ranger Rick," Bert confirmed. "We think he's been abducted by aliens."

"Well, at least he'll feel right at home." Forest shrugged half heartedly.

Sailor petted Sprinkles. "Poor puppy. Do you think she'll be alright?"

"We're on our way to the vet now to have her paw examined," Sadie stated.

"Before you leave, I have a few more questions if that's okay." I didn't want to jump to conclusions. "Exactly where were you when you found the walkie-talkie?"

"Now, let's see ..." Sadie tapped her chin. "We had just left the concession stand ... Sprinkles needed an ice cream tweet, didn't you little Sprinky?"

I started getting nauseous; worried all those pancakes would come back up.

"Then we let Sprinkles go for a swim. After that we took the beach path up to the sand dunes." She paused, fanning herself with her hands, her voice quaking. "Sprinkles ran over to the uprooted tree, began digging up the walkie-talkie, and that's when she was attacked."

"Yeah but what about the ranger—how do you know he's really missing?" I pressed them for information.

"First off, when I went to the office I asked where Ranger Rick was so I could give him back his walkie-talkie," Bert recounted. "The other rangers say to me, 'We were going to come by and ask you the same thing. He didn't show up for work today.'"

"Yes, and he never misses a day of work," Sadie added. "They tried contacting him every which way, but he seems to have disappeared."

"Alright, calm down everyone." Windsong held out her hands. "I'm sure there's a reason for all this."

"We'll look into it right away. Let us know if you find out anything else," I told them.

Bert nodded, putting the golf cart in gear.

We stopped at Forest and Sailor's site to drop off our mushrooms and formulate a plan, while Windsong and GB went back to the nature center. Windsong wanted to read some of the pamphlets on mushrooms to learn which ones were safe to eat. Something about cooking dinner with the 'delicacies' over the campfire.

"I think we should head down toward the beach and retrace the Buckley's route. Maybe we'll find something in connection with the ranger's disappearance," I suggested.

Once we arrived at the picnic area, I had a good idea where to start. I showed Forest and Sailor my hiding spot on top of the dune. "Guys, remember how Mrs. Buckley said Sprinkles found the walkie-talkie by an uprooted tree? I wonder if this is the place."

The large clump of roots had unearthed a hole in the ground behind a mature oak that had toppled over and was now lying on its side. A few branches were snapped off, showing signs of a struggle nearby.

"I think you're right." Forest bent down for a closer look. "It seems like Sprinkles was digging over here. There's a pile of dirt, and claw marks … or are they hoof marks? Maybe your road hog made this pig-sty?" Forest teased.

"You're so hilarious, Forest. So, if the ranger dropped his walkie-talkie over here, then where did he end up next?" I glanced around the area.

"Hey, check it out—something really messed up the grass down there." Sailor pointed to an open area on the other side of the ridge below us. The blades were folded over, forming an elaborate, symmetrical design. "Do you think Ranger Rick did all this?"

"Just how do you suppose he would make a per-fectly round pattern like that?" I asked.

"I don't know … he's really good at running in circles." Sailor twisted her braids.

Poor, sweet, single-digit IQ Sailor. God love 'er.

"Are you guys blind? That's gotta be a crop cir-cle!" Forest got up with a jerk. "I've seen ones like this on TV. Most scientists think they're made by extrater-restrials."

"Maybe the ranger really did get abducted by aliens." Sailor nervously rubbed her elbows. "Shouldn't we report this to Captain Quinn?"

"I'm pretty sure he's at some festival," I recalled. "We could call the police, but without proof that the ranger was really abducted, I doubt they'd get involved."

Right now, it was all up to us. I was beginning to wonder if we were in over our heads.

Kicking up a pile of what looked like fall foliage and brush under my feet, I felt something heavy. Bending down to get a closer look, I realized it was actually a camouflage suit covered with artificial leaves. It blended in so well that we almost missed it.

"Hey, guys—either someone was out hunting, or they were trying to get around Point Beach undetected—possibly both." I held up the suit; it was twice my size.

I checked to see if there were any pockets. Sure enough. I found an opening on the inside of the coat lining. I reached in, grabbing hold of something unusual. Flinging the odd-shaped object to the ground, I wiped off its gooey residue onto the leg of my pants.

Disgusting!

"What is that?" Sailor held her nose. "It looks like it's from another planet."

"Maybe it's some kind of mushroom. Too bad Norman left so quickly. I bet he'd know."

The gooey entity had a potent, earthy smell that was now clinging to my pants. I gingerly picked up the stinky, rock-shaped organism and wrapped it in a napkin, placing it in the inside pocket of my backpack.

Being more careful this time, I searched the other side of the suit and found another pocket, this time with a piece of paper inside. It had an address scribbled on it:

U.F.O.

2022 Washington Street, Two Rivers.

CHAPTER 7

After the recent revelations, we decided to split up. Forest and Sailor stayed behind with Windsong to get a search team together to look for Ranger Rick, while I tried to convince GB into taking a quick trip into town.

I showed him the address on the piece of paper that I found in the area where the ranger was reportedly abducted. He thought I was off my rocker to believe it had any connection with the disappearance but humored me anyway.

As we drove down Washington Street, I quickly discovered that the "U.F.O." on the note stood for "Unique Flying Objects," a store that sold kites. A scattering of windsocks and whirly kites hung outside the building, making my eyes spin in circles.

We got out and walked into the store, surprised at the different varieties and colorful collections they had in stock. GB made a beeline straight to a green and gold Green Bay Packer kite, but my eyes glued onto something bigger.

"I've never seen a kite like this before." I studied the oversized, flying saucer kite.

"It even has LED lights for flying at night." The salesman smiled, revealing a small gap between his front teeth. "This was a popular one at 'Kites over Lake Michigan' last week."

"Kites over Lake Michigan?" GB tilted his head.

"Yes." The man grabbed a brochure from behind his desk. "It takes place every year, on Labor Day weekend. We get visitors from all over."

GB put the brochure in his pocket.

Hmmm ... my eyes lit up. *What if some of the lights I saw in the sky came from an LED kite?* "Wanna buy me an early birthday present, GB? I can put ten bucks toward it." I enthusiastically pulled out my pancake-eating money.

"Sold!" GB took the kite, walking over to the counter where the salesman stood waiting.

"Hey, Mister, is there an internet café around

here by chance?" I asked, as he rang up our order.

"Well, now, there is Red Bank Coffeehouse. I don't know if it's an internet café, but they do have public access to Wi-Fi. It's just a few blocks south of here, inside Schroeder's Department Store."

"Dominic, what are you up to now? I told Windsong we'd be back in an hour to help search for Ranger Rick."

"I need to look up a few things for the case before we return to the campground's no-reception zone. That's all. I promise."

The clerk leaned toward GB. "They also happen to have the best homemade pie in town."

"Sold again!" GB said, pointing a finger in my direction. "We need to make this quick!"

When we got to the café, I ordered a hot chocolate with extra whipped cream. I politely asked the nice lady behind the counter for the internet password before joining GB at a small table near the windows where he contentedly munched on a piece of pecan pie.

After I signed in on my cell phone, I entered the

SCI-FI-WI address. It immediately loaded a ritzy page with a black, star-studded background and flashing strobe lights as links, including a list of all the UFO sightings in Wisconsin dating back fifty-some years. There was another list on the right side of the screen with video footage. I clicked on a video.

"Greetings, alien hunters. We're filming live in Two Rivers, Wisconsin, where a prominent citizen just reported seeing a peculiar light in the sky last week." Quinn turned to a tall man. The man had a moon-shaped face and black hair plastered to his head that was parted in the middle. It looked like he had too many teeth in his mouth.

"Are we on?" The tall man cleared his throat. "Hello. Last week ..."

I paused the video, scrolling down to the credits. There was a handful of names listed. Wanda Roth was credited as the new videographer. On a whim, I opened another window and googled her. There were several people that had the same name. I started going down the list, until one in particular caught my eye:

Biological chemist, Wanda Roth, descendant of former Two Rivers, Wisconsin, native, Herman Schlundt, industrial chemist known for his work with Noble Prize-winner Marie Curie in the field of radium.

Wanda's a chemist? What on earth is she doing playing tag-along to an alien hunter?

A call was coming in on my phone. I checked the number — it was Forest.

"Hey, what's up?" I answered.

"They found a flyer for Sputnikfest at the office, lying on the ranger's desk with a license plate number scribbled on it. We're headed there now. It's at the Rahr West Art Museum in Manitowoc. Can you meet us?"

"On our way …" I hung up the phone.

"Hey, Dominic, you made it!" Forest and Sailor ran over to the truck just as we arrived.

"What's Sputnikfest, anyway?" I asked.

Forest held up a flyer. "It's a festival to celebrate the day when a piece of the Soviet Sputnik spacecraft fell right onto this city street back in 1962."

"Wow, that's the same year the UFO conspiracy took place!" I looked over the flyer, noticing the penciled-in license plate #ARE-A51 at the bottom.

"Yeah, we searched the park for hours, and so far, it's our only lead," Forest admitted.

"More like one hour, but anyway, they even have a 'Ms. Space Debris' contest!" Sailor cheered. "It's like a Miss America Pageant, where you show off your talent and fashion. It's going on right now."

"Hey, Ms. Space Debris ..." Forest emptied a shoe full of sand onto her. "Maybe you could wear some debris for your evening gown. We're supposed to be looking for the plate number, not beauty queens."

Sailor held her hands in front of her eyes to block the sand. "What's wrong with you, Forest?"

"He has a point," I noted. "Stars are made out of dust. You'd look pretty authentic."

"Isn't this groovy?" Windsong lowered her straw sun hat over her eyes as we joined in on the festivities outside the Rahr West Art Museum.

A parade of characters marched our way, dressed in space suits. Some wore helmets on their heads, holding orange-tipped laser guns; others in robes carried glowing light sabers. A handful of pets trotted along in alien-themed costumes.

Next in line, a silver-paneled spacecraft came cruising toward us that looked like a flying saucer on wheels. It paused in front of the museum; a hatch opening on the roof. Out popped a mini-Martian with a painted-green body.

We stopped to watch as a myriad of aliens, storm troopers, and minions began swarming the premises. In the midst of it all was a baffled lady with blue hair, trying to make her way through the conglomeration.

It was Mrs. Buckley, wearing glittery glasses and a silver sequin top with matching leggings. She was weaving through the crowd leading Sprinkles on a leash. The poor pooch had a large, plastic cone around her head, and she was wrapped up in colorful gauze bandages.

"What are they doing here?" Sailor asked.

"Not sure, but they fit right in," Forest said, laughing. "Mrs. B's giant sunglasses and fake, spray-on tan makes her look orange as a pumpkin, and what happened to Sprinkles?"

"She probably got that from the vet," I assumed.

A voice called for attention over the sound system. It came from a man who was dressed in a uniform with straight, black hair and pointed eyebrows; a pretend ray-gun slung to his belt. "And now, it's time to announce the winner of this year's 'Ms. Space Debris' contest."

The crowd applauded. I held two fingers in my mouth, giving a loud whistle. A drum roll progressed, and a woman dressed like a warrior princess approached the table to deliver an envelope.

"Our judges have made a unanimous decision,

and the award goes to … the blue-haired Martian-lady and the furry conehead!" the man proclaimed as the crowd went wild and cheered some more.

One of the storm troopers grabbed Mrs. Buckley who was still wandering around aimlessly, escorting her to the front of the stage.

"I'm sincerely sorry, Officer," Mrs. Buckley said while the announcer held the microphone to her. "I got lost and didn't realize that I was driving the wrong way on a one-way street. Are you going to arrest me?"

The man laughed. "A well-dressed lady with a sense of humor. No Ma'am, you won the 'Ms. Space Debris' pageant."

"Really? This is such a surprise!" Mrs. Buckley stood proudly as he presented her with a cosmic crown and space-age scepter, while poor Sprinkles pawed at the cone on her head.

After Sadie stepped down from the stage, she spotted us in the crowd and weaved her way over.

"How does it feel to be this year's winner?" Sailor admired Sadie in all her splendor.

Sadie shrugged her shoulders. "I'm not sure. I don't even know how we made it here. After Bert stopped the car, I got out to ask for directions and somehow wound up in this mess, for goodness' sake."

"Congratulations, Sadie! How is Sprinkles doing?" Windsong reached over the plastic cone, mussing the poodle's mophead. "Poor thing."

"Oh, she'll be fine. Just a scrape. I dread to think what kind of creature could've done this to her—and the worst part is—it's still out there." She clutched Sprinkles closer. "What are you all doing here? Shouldn't you be looking for the ranger?"

"We're actually following a lead." Forest sighed. "So far, it's been dead-end."

GB and Windsong offered to walk Mrs. Buckley to her car and help get Bert moving in the right direction. While they were gone, we had our fill of neon-frosted planet cookies, Starburst candy, and rocket-fuel juice drinks.

As the crowd began to dissipate, I was about to call it quits, when suddenly, my ears caught a familiar sound. I looked back to find Quinn cruising out of the parking lot in his van, broadcasting his creepy space music.

The three of us listened intently as the alien synthesizer commenced and Quinn began to speak. "To top off today's episode of Sci-Fi-Wisconsin, here's a short clip of tomorrow's entertainment." A narrated recording began to play:

"The park ranger managed to escape from Point Beach but came to the horrible realization that he had been abducted by aliens."

"We altered his brain …"

A metallic, robot voice trailed off from the speaker before the van drove away. That sure sounded suspicious.

I quickly checked his license plate. ARE-A51.

It was a match!

CHAPTER 8

By the time we got back to Point Beach, the sky had turned a monotone grey, and with most of the campground deserted, it looked positively bleak.

GB met up with Windsong to continue the search for Ranger Rick, which left us some valued time to conduct a meeting.

"Hey, Dominic, your site's cool!" Sailor nodded her approval as she circled the fire pit.

"More like classic." Forest dropped into a green canvas chair. "What's to eat?"

I foraged inside Nimrod for food and was fortunate to score some pudgy pie supplies. I carried the haul to the picnic table.

"Take your pick. Ham and cheese, or blueberry."

Forest started the fire while Sailor and I buttered the bread, assembling the sandwiches. After we roasted our supper, I worked up the courage to tell them about the bizarre apparition I saw that first day on our site. For once, Forest kept his mouth shut; maybe that's because it was full of pie.

"So, yeah, I guess we have a ghost bush on this property. Anyway, I almost forgot to tell you about the clue I found on the SCI-FI-WI website." I quickly changed the subject, filling them in on the video I saw of Quinn, and Wanda's job title.

"Are you serious? Here you are, spotting pigs and flashing lights, and now you're claiming that the bushes around your campsite are moving, and the video lady is really a scientist? I don't know what to think anymore. Have you been eating too many mushrooms?" Forest wiped the blue jam from his mouth with the back of his hand.

"You're the one who made a big fuss over the mushrooms. I don't even like them." I shuddered at the thought. "It seems to me someone's going through a lot of trouble to clear out the campground. Maybe we'll learn more after I test out my kite theory."

"What theory is that, exactly?" Forest asked.

"I want to head down to the lake tonight and fly my new UFO kite. If I'm right, the LED lights should simulate a real flying saucer. It might even prove this entire alien invasion is nothing but a hoax."

"What do you make of the mushroom guy?" Sailor asked. "He really thinks there are aliens here."

"If you ask me, he's been eating the mushrooms, too," Forest joked. "Hey, Dominic, what was it that you were saying to Norman before—something about swamp gas?"

"Oh, yeah. So, the Buckleys mentioned there's swamp gas here. Since we still don't know where all the weird fog is coming from, I wondered if swamp gas can be altered to turn the air green, somehow." I started clearing off the table.

"Come to think of it," Sailor recalled, "while we searched for the ranger, we picked up litter and I found a bunch of plastic jugs that were thrown in the swamp. That might have something to do with it."

"What kind of jugs?" I asked.

"I don't know, they were covered in mud."

"Let's not forget the mission at the top of our list. We need to find Ranger Rick. If the aliens didn't abduct him, then someone else did," Forest added. "And so far, Quinn is our prime suspect."

"It seems that way, but what's the motive?" I couldn't think of any.

"To get more viewers for his YouTube show." Forest reached for a bag of potato chips. "That's my guess."

"What do you make of the license plate number on that flyer you found at the office? Do you think Ranger Rick wrote that on there?" I asked him.

"Who knows? He seemed suspicious of Quinn. Maybe he was in the middle of his own investigation on him, trying to disprove the existence of aliens."

"There you are!" GB and Windsong came sauntering into our site. GB sniffed the air. "Something smells mighty tasty. You kids been cooking?"

"We had pudgy pies," Sailor announced, "and now we're getting ready to fly Dominic's UFO kite!" She jumped up and down, nearly losing her balance.

"Slow down, Sweetheart," Windsong said. "You'll have to wait until tomorrow to fly your kite. We're supposed to get some rain later today."

"Just because some frogs were croaking?" Forest ran his hand through his hair.

"Could be. But my arthritis has the final say over weathermen and frogs." GB rubbed his knees.

"Did you all have enough to eat? We had mushroom lasagna, and there's plenty of leftovers," Windsong offered.

Forest grabbed his neck, making a choking noise in his throat.

"Is that a no, Mr. Smarty Pants?"

Suddenly, out of the corner of my eye, I saw a green haze floating in the woods behind us.

GB caught the direction of my stare. "What on earth? Where's that coming from?"

We took a short walk into the woods, mystified by the glowing fog. It rose into the air, circling in and out of the trees. Then, as suddenly as it had appeared, it vanished.

"Grandpa Bob?" Sailor's voice shook. "Do you believe there could be aliens on our planet?"

GB patted her arm. "No, dear girl. I don't. If the good Lord made a whole other species, I believe He would've told us." That seemed to calm her down.

I suddenly missed my mom. She would comfort me in this situation, if she were here. Maybe some of her chocolate chip cookies would help.

We headed back to the campfire, staring at the flames in silence until it started drizzling and we decided to call it a day.

The rain poured all night long. Stupid frogs.

CHAPTER 9

The rain finally lifted, leaving a pattern of swirling gray and black shadows in the sky. GB had set my alarm to go off before dawn, so we could try out my kite in the dark.

Forest and Sailor came over to help me get the kite ready. I spread out the black material on the picnic table, connecting the spreader wands into the struts as instructed. Then I tested the LED lights that were strung in a circular pattern around the center of the kite.

"It might be a long shot, but if I'm right, these lights should resemble the ones I saw over the lake. Let's grab our flashlights and bikes and head down to the beach."

Once we arrived, I carried the outstretched kite over the dune and onto the trail leading down to the beach. It seemed sturdy enough as I let it dangle in the gusty wind. "Okay, I'm gonna carry the kite along the shore while one of you lets out some string."

Forest took hold of the spool, releasing the line as I backed up. Once I was a good distance away, I sent the kite into the air, letting the wind take it out of my hands.

"Here goes!" I yelled, launching it up into the sky. The kite produced a spectacular light show above us. I watched the green and purple LED's flash in a circular pattern. It looked like a real flying saucer.

"This is awesome. I never flew a kite like this before." Forest stared upward.

"Let me have a try," Sailor begged.

Forest carefully handed her the spool.

"When the wind catches it and you feel the kite pulling, let a little line slip through your fingers. Then the kite will go higher," I instructed her.

Sailor started running with the kite, letting out the line as she went, her braids flying behind her.

"That's too much!" I yelled.

It went higher and higher, when suddenly the

wind shifted. The line began to sag, and the kite came crashing down—right into a tree.

Sailor stood motionless, holding the spool in her hands. "I'm sorry, Dominic."

"It's okay. I know you didn't mean for that to happen."

We found my kite in a tangled mess, lit up like a star on top of a Christmas tree. I yanked on the line a few times, but it wouldn't budge.

"At least you got to test your theory." Forest smiled sympathetically. "Now that it seems this could all just be an alien hoax, we need to figure out who's behind it."

"You know, guys, I've been doing some thinking, and ..."

"Hold on—this could take a while, let me find a seat," Forest interrupted, making himself comfortable on a log before I continued.

"This mystery totally reminds me of *Star Trek Episode IV: The Voyage Home*." I began my comparison. "It's hard to explain, but basically an alien probe is threatening life on earth. So, Captain Kirk and his crew steal a Klingon spaceship and go back in time by flying around the sun in reverse in an attempt to save the planet from future devastation."

"That tells me absolutely nothing," Forest said.

"Well, Kirk has to be careful no one will recognize them. The ship has an invisible cloaking device, and that way the crew can keep undercover while they capture two humpback whales from the zoo and bring them back into the future to communicate with the probe."

"What do whales have to do with anything?" Sailor raised her eyebrows.

"Never mind. The point is—I'm hot on the trail. I think something mysterious is going on right under our noses, and the alien invasion is a ploy to distract us from what's really going on inside the park."

"So, the leaf suit is kinda like a cloaking device?" Sailor guessed.

"Exactly!" I jumped up. "I think whoever was wearing it, is our alien inventor."

"And Ranger Rick is an evil Klingon. Okay, okay, I get it." Forest shook his head. "So now, we just need to figure out a way to catch who's responsible for all this, and try and locate the ranger," he concluded.

"I'm beginning to worry. He's been gone a long time." Sailor chewed on her fingernails.

"Right now, I'm more worried about what's for breakfast." I lifted the kickstand on my bike.

"Wait, what about the kite?" Sailor asked.

I turned to look at it again. We would need a big stick to get it down. "It can wait."

On our way back I noticed that one of the bins at the recycling center was filled to the top; a few plastic containers were keeping the lid pried open. We stopped to take a look.

"Are those the same jugs you found in the swamp?" I asked Forest and Sailor after I saw the mud that was caked on a few of them.

"I think so." Sailor squinted at the heap inside.

I took one out, rinsing it in a puddle so I could read the label. "Hmm … This container held a product called copper sulfate. The directions say it's commonly used as an herbicide, pesticide, or fungicide." I scratched my head. "Hey, you guys, I wonder if copper sulfate could cause a chemical reaction with swamp gas and create green fog?"

"Well, if a meteor containing copper creates a green streak of light, then why not?" Forest reasoned.

"I think that's a good question for a chemist," Sailor suggested.

"It sure is," I said.

Now we were really getting somewhere. The copper sulfate had to be connected to Wanda, somehow. I was so excited, I barely noticed my stomach growling. We hopped on our bikes and were about to head back, when I heard a loud banging sound coming from the other direction.

"Hold up, guys. Did you hear that?"

Forest and Sailor stopped their bikes beside me.

"Yeah, let's check it out." Forest turned his bike around. We coasted down the road, slowing to a halt along site #127 when we heard the noise again.

Clank, Clank.

"I think it's coming from inside the pumphouse." I listened closer.

Clank, Clank, Clank.

Sailor's knees started knocking together, her voice jittery. "Maybe you two should go ahead. I'll wait here. If there's trouble, I'll run for help."

"Come on, Sailor." I prodded her.

We continued up the driveway toward the pumphouse, surrounded by trees at the far end of the site. From a safe distance, I steadied my flashlight on the small structure built out of stones with logs supporting the mossy roof. Then I shined the beam over to the window, waiting to see if anything moved inside.

"Help! This is Ranger Rick! Anybody out there?"

CHAPTER 10

We stared at each other in disbelief. Could it really be Ranger Rick?

"How do we know it's you?" I yelled back.

"Don't get smart with me, Nimrod."

"It's him, alright," Sailor said. "One of us better go over there."

"Dominic's the one who wants to 'Boldly go where no man has gone before,' remember?" Forest gave me a shove toward the pumphouse.

I approached the wooden door, cautiously trying the latch. It wouldn't budge, so I went over to the window, stepping onto the bench below it to peek inside.

"What do you see?" Sailor called to me.

"The ranger's in there, alright, and he's tied up."

"Someone should've done that a long time ago," Forest smirked. "Why don't we leave him there, so he stays out of our way."

Forest had a point, but I knew that wouldn't go over very well with the snarky ranger.

Just then, a vehicle with green under glow pulled into the driveway.

"Hey! What are you kids doing?" Quinn stuck his head out the window; scanner antennas weaving back and forth from the roof after smacking a few low-hanging tree branches.

Sailor started toward the van. "Quinn! We need your help—Ranger Rick's tied up inside the pumphouse!"

"Or maybe he already knew that, Sailor!" Forest pulled her back. "This *is* his site, remember?"

"What are you talking about?" Quinn looked baffled. "Someone tied him up? Are you kidding me?"

Clank. Clank. CLANK.

"Nimrod! What's the hold up?" Ranger Rick's voice echoed from inside.

Quinn flew out of the van, leaving the door open behind him. With his help we were able to jimmy the door and get inside. Ranger Rick twisted himself around, hands and feet tightly bound. He jerked back and forth.

"Hurry and get me out of here!" he demanded, beady eyes glaring at us while Quinn and I worked quickly to untie the knots.

"How did you end up in the pumphouse?" Quinn asked, when the ranger was finally free.

"Funny you should ask, E.T., seeing as this is your site." He indignantly tore off the rest of the ropes. "Come to think of it, you threatened me! Said I would get abducted by aliens. You probably put me here!"

Quinn's jaw dropped. "No way, Ranger! I had no idea. I was at Sputnikfest the past two days, making videos for my website. The Baymont hotel offered me a free stay since I was adding footage from the lake behind their lot to my documentary. Honest—you can even talk to the manager about it."

I stepped between them. "Ranger Rick, he's telling the truth. I saw the video. It had to be someone else. What's the last thing you remember?"

"The last thing I remember, I saw a giant hog

sniffing around by the beach. I started chasing it, when something hit me hard over the head. Next thing I know, I'm left for dead, hogtied in this pumphouse."

"I could never do that—I don't have a mean bone in my body." Quinn shook his head.

"Maybe not," I said, "but you're still under a cloud of suspicion. I'm curious as to why you have a biological chemist recording your alien show. I find that pretty odd."

"Who, Wanda? Where'd you get that idea? She's a professional videographer who happens to be a big fan of my research. If you don't believe me, you can ask her yourself. She's meeting me here."

Just then, a red BMW turned into the driveway. I caught a flash of red hair, and realized it was Wanda. She was talking on her phone, but quickly finished the conversation, turning off the ignition once she saw what was going on. She ran out of her car, dropping her purse on the picnic table.

"Ranger Rick! Oh, my goodness, I just spoke to the Buckleys, and found out that everyone's been looking for you! Are you alright?" She took one look at the ropes lying at his feet, her face turning ashen. "There was a rumor you were abducted by aliens. I guess that wasn't the case."

"No, Ma'am. It wasn't aliens. Some prankster." Ranger Rick glared at Quinn. "When I get my hands on him, he'll have to answer to the authorities."

"I thought you *were* the authorities?" Forest raised his hands.

"Why don't you kids run along." The ranger started brushing the dirt off his pants. "Has anyone seen my radio?"

"The Buckleys found it and turned it in," Wanda said. "I believe it's on your desk at the office."

"So, Wanda, these kids found your name on an internet search and they say you're some kind of chemist. Is that true?" Quinn asked.

"What? Don't they realize that there are lots of people with the same name. One of them might be a chemist, but I'm just a fan of yours. That's the only rea-son I offered to help you."

"There, are you satisfied now?" Quinn's eyes flashed at us.

"Well, glad to see you're okay, Ranger, but I need to get going." Wanda scuffled toward her car. "I have work to do."

"Maybe I should come along," Quinn offered.

"Hold on, buddy boy ..." Ranger Rick stopped him. "You're coming with me to the office for questioning. I'm calling the manager at the Baymont to verify your alibi."

"I'm good. You better listen to the officer. I'll meet you back here later." Wanda revved the engine and sped off.

I mouthed, "Let's go" to Forest and Sailor. There was no time to lose.

We hopped on our bikes, following the red BMW. The car went directly to the park entrance, and came to a rolling stop with a right turn-signal blinking at the intersection. By the time we reached the end of the road, it was already out of sight.

My bike skid around the corner as we came to a

sudden halt. "Where'd she go? We were hot on her trail." I felt defeated.

"Those sports cars are pretty fast," Forest said. "She's probably long gone."

"Yeah, but I didn't hear it accelerate. Did either of you?"

"Nope." Sailor looked down the road. "So maybe Wanda turned in by the group site, and that's how we lost track of her car."

"Sailor, you're a genius!" I hugged her.

"Wow, nobody's ever said that to me before."

Leaving our bikes out of sight, we took a route through the woods to remain inconspicuous, position-ing ourselves as close to the group camping area as we could. Sure enough, something was going on up ahead. Wanda's red car was parked next to a 4x4 truck with an enclosed trailer hitched to it, where she was engaged in a conversation with Norman.

I guess he wasn't in such a big hurry to get out of here, after all.

"Ollie did real good today — brought me right to

the mother lode. Pretty soon the harvest will be finished, and we can go home." He raised a ramp on the back of the trailer.

"The sooner, the better. I think Quinn's onto me, and there's three pesky teenagers snooping around." Wanda scowled. "Oh, and you're going to love this — they found the ranger!"

"Real nice. I was hoping for more time. Now he'll be looking for us." Norman rubbed the back of his neck. "Oh, well … I had no choice. The ranger discovered Ollie and if I hadn't hit him over the head, he would've seen me in my camouflage suit. At least the flyer we planted on his desk with your galactic friend's plate number on it should throw him off our scent for a while."

"Oh, don't worry, the ranger already believes Quinn's the one who kidnapped him, but who knows for how long," Wanda mused.

Norman closed the trailer door. "That's okay. In another half hour we should be ready to head out. Try not to blow our cover. If you run into the ranger and he starts to get itchy, you know what to do."

"The only thing itchy around here is me, thanks to Sadie Buckley letting her dog get out of hand … *ah-choo!* If that little thing comes near me one more time … *AHHHH-CHOOOOO!*"

"Gesundheit." Norman handed her a tissue.

We had heard enough, and Wanda's allergy attack was the perfect time for us to leave while they were distracted. I was about to motion to Forest and Sailor that it was time to go, when an enormous pig emerged from behind the truck. It started grunting wildly, knocking Norman to the ground as he scrambled for the leash.

"Let's get out of here!" I jumped to my feet. The three of us took off running as the swine bolted in our direction, its thick, short legs moved surprisingly fast.

Forest and Sailor made it to their bikes first, but as luck would have it, I got tripped up in a gully, falling headfirst into the ditch. The pink, bristled animal caught up to me, taking hold of my backpack in its mouth, causing the side pocket to unsnap.

He rooted through my belongings with his leathery snout until he located what he wanted, then trotted across the road and into the campground, happily chomping on the mystery mushroom.

I collected my backpack, ran to my bike, and began peddling like the wind, speeding past the others.

"Dominic, do you think they saw you?" Forest called after me.

"I don't think so. Head to the park office!"

CHAPTER 11

"Please, you have to believe us. The mushroom guy and the video lady are in cahoots. They're using a pig for some kind of project. You saw the pig! This whole alien scare was a plot to empty the campground!" I pleaded with Ranger Rick, but he wouldn't budge.

"Well, it looks like you've been busier than a hill full of ants. You know, it's perfectly okay to bring your pet pig to the state park, as long as you keep it on a leash." He put his hat on his head, shutting the door.

And there you have it. Shot down. Big surprise.

"We can't just let Wanda and Norman get away with this when Quinn's taking the blame," I said.

Just then, Bert and Sadie Buckley came lumbering down the road toward us in their golf cart. GB, Windsong, and Sprinkles—still with a cone around her head—were crammed in the back, which made for a tight fit.

"Heavens, where have you been? We were worried sick." Windsong folded her hands, eyes looking heavenward as they approached.

Sailor ran over, burying herself in Windsong's arms. "We found Ranger Rick tied up in the pump house on site #127, and now Norman's pig is after us, but the ranger won't listen to a word we're saying."

Bert Buckley stomped his foot. "Tarnation! First we have aliens taking over the planet, and now pigs?" He had a wild look in his eyes.

"Honey, did you say that you found the ranger?" Sadie beamed. "Hallelujah! Our prayers were answered."

"That is good news." GB leveled his gaze at us. "But I think our grandchildren still have some explaining to do. Now, Sailor, calm down and tell us what happened."

"It's alright, GB. I can explain." I wanted to confess before things got too out of hand. "Okay, so I'm sorry I didn't tell you sooner, Grandpa, but we had to follow Wanda after she left the pumphouse. That's how we discovered she's not really working with Captain Quinn, she's working with the mushroom guy, and they have a pig doing all their dirty work. Remember, I told you about the pig?"

"They were using a night-flying kite with LED lights, to trick people into believing it was a UFO so they could clear out the campground. They even had Captain Quinn fooled," Forest said.

Suddenly, I had a pretty good idea what the real conspiracy was.

"Think about it … Norman's into mushrooms, and then there was a weird-looking mushroom that I found in a camouflage suit, which I stuffed in my backpack, and the pig goes bonkers over it …"

GB held his hands over his face. "You kids should know better than to go spying on dangerous criminals without coming to me first."

I looked down at my feet. He was right, as usual. This was too much for us to handle.

We were still discussing the case when Ranger Rick opened the office door, escorting Quinn outside.

"You're free to go, but remember ..." The ranger pointed two fingers at his squinty eyes, and then over to Quinn. "I've got my eyes on you."

"You may want to give him a break," Windsong demanded. "I think the children were telling the truth."

"Well, aren't you just a ray of sunshine? Now I have an entire day's worth of work to make up, and I can't waste any more time."

"Before you say one more word, take a look at this." Windsong pulled a magazine with the title *Exotic Mushroom Farming* out of her satchel. "When Bobby and I were at the nature center, I found this magazine with Norman's name and address on it. Did you know that pigs are used to hunt truffles?"

"What's that you say about waffles?" Bert leaned in closer.

"Truffles, truffles!" Sadie yelled into Bert's ear.

"Like chocolates?"

"Like mushrooms!" We all yelled.

"And they're worth a fortune," Windsong added.

Instantly, the hair on Sprinkle's back stood up. She began growling as she trotted across the lot toward something that was creating a ruckus in the woods.

"Ah … Ahh …"

"Watch out, everyone," Sailor announced as Wanda emerged from the tree line, "she's gonna blow!"

"AH-CHOO!" Wanda sneezed; the truffle she was carrying fell to the ground and began rolling toward the ranger.

He bent over and picked it up, turning it over in his hand. "Truffles don't happen to look like this, do they?"

"Ranger, look out!" GB warned, as Ollie burst through the bushes, but the hog was too quick. He knocked Ranger Rick off his feet, grabbing the truffle right out of his hand. Sprinkles began chasing the pig around the parking lot.

"Sprinkles! Oh, no!" Sadie hit the pig over the head with her purse while GB and Windsong hurried to her aid.

Bert rushed to the golf cart. "I'll get 'em." He revved the engine, frightening Ollie. The pig squealed, taking off in the other direction.

"Bert, have you lost your marbles!" Sadie cried. "You're going the wrong way." She covered her eyes.

Ranger Rick finally got up off the ground, fumbling to get his hat back on. "Don't anybody move. I'll get my gun." He ran inside the office just as a 4x4 truck and trailer drove up to the check-in lane.

"It's the mushroom man!" I shouted.

Norman took one look at all of us, then stepped on the gas, plowing through the lot at full speed. He tried to make a sharp U-turn toward the exit, but the trailer was too wide. It jackknifed between the flagpole and Bert's golf cart.

By this time, Ranger Rick had come back out and was wildly waving his rifle in the air, which caused Norman to shrink down behind the driver's wheel. Sadie was holding Sprinkles, and Wanda took off after the pig.

Since the whole place was going crazy, I signaled

Forest and Sailor to join me. We raced over to the cab, taking a peek through the window.

Well, well. What do we have here?

"Ranger, their truck is full of truffles," I said.

CHAPTER 12

"Alright, Mister. Let's have a look-see." Ranger Rick walked to the back of the truck and waited; impatiently tapping his foot.

Norman grabbed a keychain from his pocket, hesitantly unlocking the back hatch to open it. The ranger reached in, lifting a brown tarp that covered a half-dozen wooden crates filled to the brim with tubular-shaped truffles.

"It's over, Wanda," Norman said, as she brought the pig back and tied him to a tree. Her shoulders sagged as she walked over to join him.

"So, what now? Are we going to jail?"

Ranger Rick straightened his posture, legs spread. "It's against the law to destroy, molest, deface or remove any natural growth from a state park. So, there's that. Now you add the charge of kidnapping …" He narrowed his eyes at Norman and Wanda. "My guess is the two of you could be looking at time in the pen."

"The pig pen?" Forest couldn't resist.

"Watch it, Illi-noyance." Ranger Rick glared at him, then directed Norman and Wanda to take a seat while he called for backup.

"What's going to happen to that awful pig?" Sadie clucked, walking over with Sprinkles in her arms.

"I'm working on it right now." Ranger Rick lowered the phone from his face. "The petting farm at the Manitowoc Zoo should be the perfect place."

"If that doesn't work out, we could fry him into bacon," Forest cracked.

"Absolutely not," Windsong objected.

Wanda blew her nose into a tissue. "I knew getting that swine was a bad idea. You couldn't find anything with a smaller appetite, Norman?"

"What else could I do? You're allergic to dogs, and pigs have been hunting truffles for centuries," he argued. "With a muzzle on, he's really a gentle beast.

You didn't give him a chance."

Ollie grunted, sitting up on his back haunches.

"I have a question." I stepped toward them.

"About mushrooms?" Norman lifted his head.

"No, about copper sulfate."

"That was Wanda's idea," he said. "She's the brains of the operation. I'm just the good looks."

"Oh, shut up, Norm." Wanda glared at him. "I wasn't expecting a bunch of kids to go snooping around and sabotage all my plans."

"At first, we thought it was Quinn putting on the alien light show, until Sailor found the empty copper sulfate jugs in the swamp." I stared at Wanda. "That's how you made the swamp gas turn green, isn't it?"

Quinn frowned at her. "You really are a chemist, and not a videographer like you said you were?"

"Sorry, Captain Quinn," she scoffed. "SCI-FI-WI was just an easy way for me to get free publicity. At least you got some great videos for your documentary."

"I hate to break it to you, but you may not want

96

to quit your day job." Quinn crossed his arms. "A monkey could get better footage."

"So, the meteor gave you the perfect opportunity to scare people from Point Beach," Forest stated. "All you needed was to exaggerate things a little, making everyone believe it signaled an alien invasion."

"What about the crop circle we found near the beach?" Sailor asked Wanda. "How did you pull that off? It looked so real!"

"Crop circle?" Wanda tilted her head. "I don't know anything about that."

"And to think, you did all this just to make money with mushrooms?" GB wagged his index finger at them.

"You don't understand. These truffles are one of a kind—you won't find them anywhere else in the world!" Norman retorted.

"Norman!" Wanda shot him a warning look.

"What's the use. We're going to jail anyway." He shrugged. "We discovered an exotic fungus growing in this park, which we believe has anti-aging properties.

It's very unusual for truffles to grow here, but the surrounding swampland and possibly the nearby Point Beach nuclear plant have played a part in their growth."

Two squad cars pulled into the office parking lot. Ranger Rick spoke with the officers for a few minutes, leading them over to Wanda and Norman. "Give these two what they deserve!" he said, rubbing his hand over the goose egg on his head.

"We're not on a get-rich-quick scheme like you think. We were only trying to bring the fountain of youth to the world …" Norman called out, before the officers read them their rights and handcuffed them.

Ollie was loaded into a trailer. Maybe someday we could visit him at the zoo.

Ranger Rick stood with his hands on his hips. "Alright, everyone, the show's over. You can go back to your picnics." He strutted to the office, giving a nod and saluting in our direction before heading in.

"He's a piece of work," Forest mumbled.

"Sorry, Windsong. It looks like your new friend

is going to jail." GB smiled impishly.

"Bobby!" Windsong laughed, giving him a playful pinch. "Norman wasn't my friend, just a kindred spirit. Besides, I only have room in my life for real friends like you—good, honest folk."

GB's ears turned red. "Glad to hear that, Windsong. The feeling's mutual."

Any more of this chitchat and I'd be comatose.

CHAPTER 13

There was a peaceful feeling around the campfire that night. The stars were blinking, the moon was full, and the pines seemed more at ease without the toxic gases and laser lights painting the scene. The Buckleys had invited us all over for refreshments. Even Quinn dropped by.

"I'm still in shock as to how this UFO mystery ended up," Sadie said. "Great work, kids."

"It was quite the conspiracy." Sailor slurped lemonade through a straw.

"Tell me about it," Quinn said with a pained stare. "I've got video footage on my website of fake lights and fog, and nothing to show for it. My reputation is ruined."

Sadie put her hand on Quinn's shoulder. "Not so, Quirk. Your followers are faithful. There will be plenty more alien conspiracies for you to investigate."

Quinn looked alarmed. Sadie's habit of calling people whatever names popped into her head was   foreign to him.

"I'll tell you about a conspiracy," Bert interjected. "Back in 1962, my father saw a UFO in his field. He saw it, and no one believed him!" Bert slapped his knee. "The aliens are real. You'll see … you'll see," he said, shaking his head.

"So, there was a UFO, and then Bert was born. You do the math," Forest whispered in my ear. I stifled a chuckle.

"I'd love to conduct an interview with you for my documentary," Quinn proposed, handing Bert his card. "And it would be really cool if I could include the clip I caught with my dash cam, of you doing a wheelie in your golf cart in pursuit of that giant pig."

"I'd pay to see that!" I high-fived Quinn.

"By the way, do any of you kids want a kite? I found one on the beach while I was following an abnormal object on my radar." Quinn pulled out the kite from the back of the van.

"Hey, yeah, that's mine. Thanks for getting it

down." I reached for the kite.

"Well, kid, it's been a blast, but I have to get going." Quinn lifted his right hand straight upward, giving a "Vulcan salute" by separating his thumb and middle two fingers.

"You're a *Star Trek* fan?"

"Trekkie to the core." Quinn winked.

"Me too!" I held up my hand, palm flat, struggling to get my fingers to match Quinn's. "Live long and prosper." We exchanged farewells before he drove away, probably off to find new, uncharted territory to explore.

"Oooh, I ate way too much." Sailor took one last bite of her maple s'more, leaning back in her chair. "I wish we didn't have to leave tomorrow," she moaned.

"I hear you. I'm depressed just thinking about going back to school," I said. "It will feel strange to go from an outdoor adventure back to math and history classes. But I do miss Mom and Pedro."

GB reached for a log from Bert's wood pile, tossing it into the fire. "You kids have nothing to feel sad about. If it weren't for you, this campground would be a ghost town, as Dominic feared."

"Yeah, that's true!" Forest smiled. "And the ranger would still be tied up in the pumphouse." He seemed cheerful at the thought.

"And I have another surprise for you!" Windsong swirled her gypsy skirt full circle. "I brought along some paper lanterns that I made, and this would be the perfect time to launch them. What do you say we end the night at the beach?"

We waved goodbye to Mr. and Mrs. Buckley, grabbed our flashlights and paper lanterns and headed for the lake. We had just reached the field at Ridges Trail, when we came across a disfiguration in the long grass.

"Lord, this seems to be a crop circle. I heard about these." GB bent down to get a closer look.

"Another one? Are you kidding me?" Sailor swallowed hard.

The large, intricate design was a duplicate of the flattened circle we saw near the beach, but if Norman and Wanda didn't do this ... who or what did?

I turned to Forest and Sailor. "Now that we have proof that extraterrestrials may exist, how can we leave Point Beach without solving the mystery?"

"Dominic." Windsong stopped in her tracks. "You kids did solve the mystery. As for the crop circles ... it's a great big universe. There are mysteries even the most brilliant scientists don't have answers for. We just need to accept that there isn't an answer to every question, at least not on this side of heaven."

Windsong was beginning to sound like Spock. Maybe she's been reading my comics ...

The beach was deserted beneath the full moon; a sprinkling of stars lit the blackened sky. We sat by the shore on Windsong's patchwork blanket, the crashing waves breaking the silence.

"I'm cold!" Sailor huddled close to Windsong, shivering from the lake breeze.

GB began picking up sticks, tossing them in a heap on the sand in front of us.

"Bobby, are you building a fire? You know it's

probably against the rules to have a fire on the beach."

"Yeah, I figured." He took a lighter out of his pocket. "But since the campground's deserted, I don't see the harm, as long as we clean up when we're done."

GB was a Boy Scout at heart. He had a cozy fire going in no time. The branches began to crackle; flames leaping as the fire took hold.

Forest was in another world, playing games on his phone, while I stared up at the sky, thinking about aliens and UFO's.

"Just what do you think you're doing?"

A dark figure shining a flashlight approached us. With that nasal-tone voice, it had to be Ranger Rick.

"Now, Ranger," GB stood to his feet, "we're just having a harmless little fire here. Why don't you be a good sport and leave us be."

"Leave you be?!" The ranger's voice raised an octave. "You know there are rules here, fella. No fires allowed on the beach," he fumed.

"Ranger Rick?" Windsong said, softly. "I can't

imagine how frazzled you must be after the ordeal you've been through, being kidnapped, and all. These kids really look up to you, and we were all so happy they found you alive and well."

"Yes … Ma'am …" he mumbled, looking down at the sand.

He seemed to be crumbling under Windsong's influence. But then his posture stiffened; his shoulders went back as he regained composure.

"Now, make sure this fire is completely extinguished before you leave. If I find even one hot ember here in the morning, you'll be hearing from me." He swiveled around, making his way back down the beach.

"Well, I'll be, Windsong. You charmer, you." GB rubbed the white hair that finally came in on his goatee.

"Sometimes a person just needs to hear a kind word. It does wonders," she said, reaching for her beach bag. "What do you say we end this night with a blaze of glory?" She handed each of us a paper lantern.

GB used his lighter to ignite a flame onto our wicks.

We lit our lanterns, sending them floating up into the air. We watched while they took flight, rising higher and higher, flickers of fire adding lights to the starlit sky. Where they would travel to and where they would land remains a mystery, but I've come to learn … that's life—it's a mystery.

Debby lives in Maribel, Wisconsin. She's a member of Pens of Praise Christian writers' group and enjoys family gatherings, country life and the four seasons.

Kate lives in Branch, Wisconsin. She's a member of Pens of Praise Christian writers' group and a church accompanist. She enjoys spending time with her family.

Connect with us online at:

Facebook.com/MysteryatPointBeach

Facebook.com/TheTinCanSeries

We would like to thank Anne Bender and Sarah Grosskopf for their insight, Ed Specht for his *Star Trek* knowledge, Isaac Mugerwa for designing our website.

Books in the Mystery at Point Beach Series:

Book 1: Sundae Wars

Book 2: Pirate's Booty

Book 3: Alien Invasion

Book 4: Bushwhacked

Book 5: The Ringmaster

Book 6: Haunted Hemlock

Books in The Tin Can Series:

Book 1: Mystery at Flamingo Bay

Reviews for Mystery at Point Beach

"No matter your age, you are sure to get caught up in the fun and excitement as Dominic and his friends are back at Point Beach State Forest for another mysterious adventure. The characters that we've come to know and love from the first two books in this series continue to charm readers and bring joy to the heart. I can't get enough of these stories filled with local lore and escapades!"

~ Anne Bender

"Debby and Kate's books provide fun for all ages; full of adventure, humor, surprise, and even educational moments as the characters explore mysteries in real, local settings.
As always, the 'feel-good' ending leaves the reader looking forward to the next book!"

~ Sarah Grosskopf

In memory of:

"Ollie" the pig